EVERY PR
Has A
Solution

Written by Christina Torres
Illustrated by Rifai Suhganda

Thinking Mats Publishing

Thinkingmats.com

It was the very first day of school,
and in Ms. Torres' class you could hear
Miles screaming across the room.

"Hey, Liliana, you give that back!!"

Liliana said," I will not give that back, you took it from me. It's mine, mine, mine!"

Miles was so frustrated and so mad that he let out a big, "Ahhhhhhh!"

Their teacher, Ms. Torres, walked right over and said, "Liliana, Miles, it sounds like you both have a problem and we must come up with a solution."

Miles said,
"Ms.Torres, what's a problem?"

Liliana said,
"Yeah, and what's a solution?"

Ms. Torres quickly gathered the whole class together on the rainbow rug, and asked all her students what they thought a problem and solution were.

One of her students, Penny, quickly chimed in and said, "A problem is when kids don't get along. Like you two."

Cameron interjected and said,
"Noooo, it's when your mommy
gets really really mad."

Penny said, "No, it's not."
Cameron said, "Yes, it is."
"No, it's not."
"Yes, it is."
"No!"
"Yeeeessss!"
"Noooooo!"
"Yes, it IS IS IS!"

Penny said,
jumping up and down.

"Ok, ok, ok. Everyone settle down. Did you know that kids are the best kind of problem solvers?"

"Really?" her class said. They were all stunned, they couldn't believe it.

Izzy raised her hand and asked, "Ms. Torres, do you mean we are better problem solvers than teachers?" "Uh-huh!"

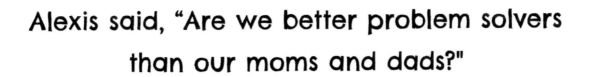

Alexis said, "Are we better problem solvers than our moms and dads?"

"What about my big sister?" said Hailey.

Ms. Torres confidently said, "Yep!" Kids are the best kind of problem solvers!"

"WOW!" said Ms. Torres' whole class. "Wow!"

Soon after, the students in
Ms. Torres' class began chanting "Woohoo!
We are the best!
We are the best!
We are the best!"

All of a sudden, the principal walked in and asked, "Ms. Torres, what's all the ruckus in here?"

"My students just realized they are the best problem solvers."

Amado jumped up and said, "Yeah! Ms. Torres told us we are the best problem solvers in the whole wide world!"

"That's right!" She nodded her head up and down.

Izzy whispered into Amado's ear, "But Ms. Torres didn't teach us how..."

Amado said, "Don't worry, I bet Ms. Torres..." And before Amado could finish his sentence, Ms. Torres went digging in her big tall closet, and boy was that closet full!

Just then, Ms. Torres popped out and pulled out a rolled-up yoga mat.

"Ah, here it is!" With that look in her eye, the students knew Ms. Torres had a plan and it was bound to be good.

"Ok, students,

I am going to show you a way for

all of us to solve our problems.

Alexis turned to her friend Kallie and said, "How in the world are we going to solve our problems with yoga?"

Kallie said, "Yeah, our teacher sounds a little crazy."

Hailey replied, "Yeah, she is always thinking of crazy ways to make learning fun! Hehehe!"

"Students, this is our problem solving mat."

"Ooooooh, aooaaah! That looks fun."

"Yes, solving problems with each other can be fun. It also helps our brain grow."

"Cool!"

"Here is step 1. This is where you will start when you have a problem.

Step 2 is where you will touch or tell how you are feeling,

and in Step 3, you will work together to figure out how to solve your problem."

"Liliana, Miles, would you like to show everyone how it's done?"

Miles and Lily both stood up and walked over to the mat and stood facing each other at step 1 while the whole class watched.

Liliana went first, "Miles, you took my favorite stuffy. I was playing with it."

Miles said, "Yeah, well I like that stuffy too. I wanted to build a castle for him but you took it."
Ms. Torres, said, "Great job! Now head over to step 2."

"You made me feel..." Miles carefully looked over all the emojis in square 2, and then he pointed and continued, "You made me feel like this and this."

Lily leaned over and saw that Miles pointed at the frustrated face and mad face.

Lily went next and she, too, carefully looked over the emojis and pointed and said, "You made me feel, mad and sad!"

Miles slowly picked his head up and looked at Lily's face and said, "I made you mad and sad? I didn't mean to make you sad."

Lily's head was down and a tear fell gently from her face. "Yeah, it hurt my feelings."

"Uh, I'm sorry Liliana."

When they heard Miles apologize to Lily, Caden blurted out, "Good job, Miles! You are doing great! Go to step 3."

At the same time, Miles and Liliana
both moved over to step 3.
"Ok, Liliana, how are we going to solve our problem?"

Liliana said, "I don't know. How about if I just use the stuffy and you use it next time?"

"Well, I want to use the stuffy too. How about if we take turns using the stuffy?"

"Ok, but who gets to go first?"
"I know, let's rock-paper-scissors?"
"Yeah, let's do it."

The class said with glee, "Yay! Lily and Miles solved their problem!"

"Welp, you did say kids are the best kind of problem solvers!" Caden declared.

"Yes, Caden, they are," said Ms. Torres with
a big smile on her face and a wink in her eye.